THE RACE OF A LIFETIME

BY TONY NORMAN

ILLUSTRATED BY PAUL SAVAGE

Librarian Reviewer
Joanne Bongaarts
Educational Consultant
MS in Library Media Education, Minnesota State University, Mankato
Teacher and Media Specialist with Edina Public Schools, MN, 1993–2000

Reading Consultant
Elizabeth Stedem
Educator/Consultant, Colorado Springs, CO
MA in Elementary Education, University of Denver, CO

▼▼ STONE ARCH BOOKS
Minneapolis   San Diego

First published in the United States in 2007
by Stone Arch Books,
151 Good Counsel Drive, P.O. Box 669,
Mankato, Minnesota 56002.
www.stonearchbooks.com

Originally published in Great Britain in 2002
by Badger Publishing Ltd.

Original work copyright © 2002 Badger Publishing Ltd
Text copyright © 2002 Tony Norman

The right of Tony Norman to be identified as the author
of this work has been asserted by him in accordance
with the Copyright, Designs and Patent Act 1988.

Library of Congress Cataloging-in-Publication Data
Norman, Tony.
    The Race of a Lifetime / by Tony Norman; illustrated by Paul Savage.
    p. cm. — (Keystone books.)
    Summary: Thirteen-year-old Jamie's younger sister helps him prepare
for the bicycle race he has been daydreaming about.
    ISBN-13: 978-1-59889-093-8 (hardcover)
    ISBN-10: 1-59889-093-X (hardcover)
    ISBN-13: 978-1-59889-249-9 (paperback)
    ISBN-10: 1-59889-249-5 (paperback)
    [1. Bicycle racing—Fiction. 2. Brothers and sisters—Fiction.]
I. Savage, Paul, 1971–, ill. II. Title.
PZ7.N7862Rac 2007
[Fic]—dc22   2006004058

1 2 3 4 5 6 11 10 09 08 07 06

Printed in the United States of America

TABLE OF CONTENTS

CHAPTER 1

The Daydream

Jamie could see the finish line high above him at the top of a steep, muddy hill.

There was so much noise, Jamie couldn't think. Teachers, parents, and kids from school, all staring at him.

He felt the sweat run down his face.

Jamie was pumping the pedals of his bike like crazy, but he felt like he was stuck in one spot.

"What is this?" he kept asking himself. "What's going wrong?"

Then he heard a voice, through a loudspeaker. "And here's Jamie Collins, riding the oldest bike in the race. Better late than never, Jamie!"

The truth hit Jamie like a smack in the face. The people on the hill weren't cheering. They were laughing, laughing at him and his silly old bike.

Jamie felt a burst of anger deep inside.

He pedaled faster and faster.

He had just one thought in mind. I must finish the race. I must finish the race. I must finish the . . .

"Oh! Look out!" A delivery man walking nearby looked angry.

Jamie swerved and slid to a stop.

"You have to be more careful, son," the man said.

Jamie stared at him.

A delivery man? What was he doing here?

Then Jamie's mind jumped back to the real world, back to Friday morning, back to his paper route.

Now he understood. The laughing faces were just in his mind.

"Sorry," said Jamie. "I was just thinking about something."

"Daydreaming!" said the man. He climbed into his truck and drove off.

Jamie felt angry. He jumped off his old bike and kicked it.

"Piece of old junk!" he shouted. Then he kicked the bike again.

What chance did he have to win the school race on that old thing?

Jamie's mind was made up. He knew what he had to do.

CHAPTER 2

BUZZING

When Jamie got home, he tried to talk to his dad. It wasn't easy. The kitchen was full of people.

Jamie was 13. He had two younger sisters and two younger brothers. Sometimes he felt like they all came from another planet.

Jamie's youngest sister's name was Sharon. She was nine, but she seemed older. She was sitting by herself at the computer.

Jamie's mom kept giving time checks, like a DJ on the radio.

"Come on everyone, it's ten to eight," she shouted above the noise.

Jamie's dad was playing his guitar and singing. His voice made Jamie think of stray cats howling in the dead of night.

When his dad stopped to take a bite of toast, Jamie took his chance.

"I want a mountain bike for the school race," he said.

"Who's going to pay for it?" Dad asked.

"Me. I've been saving up from my paper route," said Jamie.

"Well, sure then, that's cool," Dad said. He smiled. "Nice one, Jamie. Go for it!"

Jamie hated it when his dad tried to sound cool, but this time it didn't matter.

Jamie was buzzing inside.

CHAPTER 3

S-ZONE

That night, Jamie went on the Internet to find out how much a mountain bike would cost. Every website gave him the same bad news. Jamie hardly had enough cash to buy a new wheel, let alone a new bike.

"Don't stay on there too long," called his mom.

Jamie didn't argue. He quickly checked his e-mail.

There was one message in his inbox.

| To: Jamie |
| From: s-zone |
| Date: April 8 |
| Subject: Cool Bike |

Hi Jamie,

See local paper. For sale. Page 16.
Do it now.

s-zone

Jamie sat back and stared at the screen. He had no idea who the e-mail was from, but he decided to check it out.

He found the local paper. He saw the ad for the used bike. He made the call. He spoke to the boy who was selling it.

The first thing next morning, Jamie saw the bike. It was a little rusty and had lots of dents and scratches.

That didn't matter to him. The main thing was that the bike was cheap, a price Jamie could afford. So, he decided to buy it.

Jamie was happy, but he still kept asking himself the same question.

Who was s-zone?

CHAPTER 4

SELFISH

The big race was just two weeks away. There were posters all over school.

When Jamie thought about the race, his heart beat faster. He had to get his bike ready in time. He spent every spare minute working on it in the garage.

IT'S PEDAL POWER !

race of a lifetime

JULY 20TH

Sharon, his sister, started hanging around. At first, she got on Jamie's nerves, but he soon saw she could be useful.

Sharon didn't seem to mind what she did, as long as Jamie let her help.

They both worked hard.

Jamie took the bike apart. He worked on the frame. The dents and scratches were small. He soon fixed them. Then he painted the frame jet black. It looked really cool.

Sharon washed the mud off the tires. They were as good as new. Then she got all the rust off the wheels and painted them silver.

One week later, Jamie's bike was ready to ride.

His mom said they had to go to the local bike shop first for a safety check. Mom paid, so Jamie didn't mind.

The man in the shop checked the brakes and the gear change. He said the bike was fine. Jamie's mom bought him a helmet, elbow-pads, and knee-pads. Jamie put them on. Sharon said he looked good, but Jamie wasn't listening to her.

Before they left, the man set the seat to just the right height for Jamie.

Now the bike was perfect and Jamie was on top of the world.

"Can I try your bike later?" said Sharon. Her voice was small and timid.

"No you can't!" snapped Jamie. "Try my bike when it's all set up for the race? Are you crazy?"

Sharon didn't say a word, but her face turned red.

"Jamie," said his mom, in a hurt voice, "that isn't nice after all Sharon's done for you."

Jamie left his mom and Sharon at the shop.

He rode home alone.

The bike was great, but Jamie felt sick inside. He kept seeing Sharon's sad face. Why had he shouted at her like that?

"Jamie, you're a selfish rat!" he said out loud and pedaled harder and faster, all the way home.

One hour later, Jamie's mom's cell phone beeped. She read the text message.

"I think this is for you, honey," she said to Sharon.

"What does it say?" asked Sharon.

"You read it," said Mom, handing her the phone.

The message was short and sweet:

```
u r my coach ok?
```

Sharon knew who the text was from.

CHAPTER 5

GO FOR IT!

Jamie knew he'd been mean to Sharon. He wanted to make up for it now, but did he really want her to be his coach? No, of course not.

The way Jamie saw it, he'd do some training for the 'Race of a Lifetime' and Sharon could come and watch, simple as that.

Sharon had other ideas. They did not have long to train, so she'd make sure Jamie worked very hard!

Training started on Monday, after school. Jamie had a map of where the bikes would race in the park. He did a test lap around the track.

"Do it again," said Sharon. "This time, when you get to that last hill, go for it!"

Jamie looked at Sharon. She was a tough coach, but what she said made sense.

So, he got back on his bike and tried again.

Tuesday. Wednesday. Thursday. Every training session was better than the last.

"Nice one!" said Sharon after the last lap on Thursday. She smiled. "Best time yet, by nine seconds. You can win this race, Jamie. You can really win it!"

"I still hate racing up that hill," said Jamie.

"We'll work on it," said Sharon. "Nothing can stop us now."

But she was wrong!

CHAPTER 6

NIGHTMARE

Friday morning. 7:34 a.m.

That's when Jamie's world caved in.

He came out of an apartment building on his paper route and stared in horror.

His bike had been stolen. He couldn't believe it was happening, but it was.

The rest of Friday was like a bad dream.

Sharon helped Jamie look for his bike. They searched all over town. They asked every kid they met, but nobody knew a thing. It was hopeless.

Jamie felt so bad, he didn't want to get up on Saturday.

Sharon told him he was a wimp. He knew she was right, so they went to watch the race together. Suddenly, Sharon ran off through the crowd.

"That's my brother's bike, you thief!" Sharon shouted at a tough boy who was twice her size.

She tried to take the bike, but the boy pushed her away. Jamie didn't like that.

He grabbed the bike from the boy and gave him a hard look. The boy's dad stormed up to them.

"What's going on?" he shouted.

Sharon wasn't afraid. She turned the bike upside down and pointed to some silver letters painted under the saddle. They read: s-zone.

"That's my e-mail name," said Sharon. "Ask my mom if you don't believe me. I put it there for luck when I helped Jamie paint this bike. Your son stole it."

The sly boy turned red. His dad dragged him away, without another word.

Jamie was in shock.

"You're s-zone?" he said to Sharon.

"Better get over it, Jamie," Sharon said, smiling. "You're back in the race!"

CHAPTER 7

WINNER OR LOSER?

The race flew past in a blur. Jamie was a blaze of energy. Down the hill he rushed, over the bridge, and back across the small stream. His legs felt strong as he pedaled fast across the long, flat field beside the line of trees.

The race was almost over and Jamie was in the lead. He could see the finish line high above him, at the top of the steep, muddy hill. Now, for the final test!

Jamie stood up and pedaled as hard as he could.

The noise of the crowd filled his ears. Were they cheering, or laughing at him, like in his dream?

Don't think about it, he told himself, but it was too late.

Another bike zipped into the lead. Mud from its wheels flew up in Jamie's face. Jamie knew he had lost.

The rider in the lead was closing in on the finish line. He put one hand in the air and waved to the crowd. Then his foot slipped off a muddy pedal. His bike twisted to the right and Jamie was past him and over the line in a flash.

Jamie couldn't believe it.

He'd won!

"Okay, folks, let's hear it for our 'Race of a Lifetime' champion, Jamie Collins!" said a voice from the loudspeaker.

"Hold the cup up, Jamie," yelled the photographer from the local paper.

Jamie saw Sharon in the crowd.

"Come on!" he yelled to her above the cheers.

Posing for the photos felt good, like being a star or something. Sharon held one side of the cup and Jamie held the other.

There were smiling faces all around. Then Jamie gave Sharon a present.

It was his gold medal for winning the race.

"It's yours," Jamie said with a big smile. "Couldn't have won it without you, coach!"

ABOUT THE AUTHOR

Tony Norman is a children's writer and poet from the South Coast of England. He once played in a band in a school talent show. Tony still sings and plays guitar. Loyal fans include the frogs, toads, and fish in his garden pond!

ABOUT THE ILLUSTRATOR

Paul Savage works in a design studio. He says illustrating books is "the best job." He's always been interested in illustrating books, and he loves reading. Paul also enjoys playing sports and running.

He lives in England with his wife and their daughter, Amelia.

daydreaming (DAY-dreem-ing)—wishing or thinking about pleasant things that one would like to happen

DJ (DEE-jay)—a disc jockey; someone who chooses and plays records or CDs for a radio station, disco, or party

selfish (SEL-fish)—concerned about oneself and not thinking of others

sly (SLYE)—sneaky or tricky

stormed (STORMD)—moved angrily

stray (STRAY)—lost

swerve (SWURV)—to turn quickly and sharply

DISCUSSION QUESTIONS

1. At the end of Chapter Two, on page 11, it says, "Jamie was buzzing inside." What does that mean? How did he feel?

2. Why did Sharon send Jamie an e-mail about the bike for sale? Why didn't she just tell him?

3. Why didn't Jamie just fix up his old bike?

4. Why did Sharon want to help Jamie?

WRITING PROMPTS

1. What is the point of this story? Is it about a bike race? Is it about a brother and sister's relationship? Is it about winning? Explain what you think this story is really about and why.

2. Why is this book titled "The Race of a Lifetime"? What title would you give it? Why?

3. What happens to the relationship between Jamie and Sharon in this book? Does it change? How does it change? Why does it happen?

ALSO BY TONY NORMAN

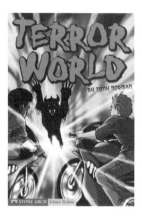

Terror World

Jimmy and Seb love playing the arcade games at Terror World. When the owner offers them a free trial on a new game, they enter the real "Terror World." Chased by Razor Cats, it seems there is no escape.

Nervous

Elite is the best band in school. The Dream Stars Talent Show gives Jools and Cass the chance to prove their band is just as good, or even better.

The Bombed House
by Jonny Zucker

During World War II Ned and Harry Jennings find something very strange at 46 Willow Street. The only problem is, no one believes what they have discovered.

The Reactor
by J. Powell

When Joe and his friends are locked out of The Reactor, an abandoned building they have claimed as their own, they set out to uncover the sinister activities of the building's mysterious new owners.

INTERNET SITES

Do you want to know more about subjects related to this book? Or are you interested in learning about other topics? Then check out FactHound, a fun, easy way to find Internet sites.

Our investigative staff has already sniffed out great sites for you!

Here's how to use FactHound:

1. Visit *www.facthound.com*

2. Select your grade level.

3. To learn more about subjects related to this book, type in the book's ISBN number: **159889093X**.

4. Click the **Fetch It** button.

FactHound will fetch the best Internet sites for you!